GW00496940

FOUR: A Novella

P.J. Blakey-Novis

Four: A Novella

For Leanne, as always, my biggest supporter

The Four

Camping. Despite the unpredictable British weather, camping remains a firm favourite for a few days escape from reality. And along with this, a few traditions are adhered to. Who can resist the opportunity to mess around with alcohol and fire? What could be more enjoyable than eating meat from a portable grill, with a choice of cremated or dangerously pink in the middle? Or burning marshmallows to the point that the roof of one's mouth blisters upon impact? Or attempting to frighten one another with tales of terror, as the flames cut through the solid darkness of night in the countryside? And that is surely the best part. Yes, camping, like any other getaway, provides an escape from daily life. But it also provides an escape from the *safety* of daily life. The protection of one's house or flat is now gone. You are exposed, not just to the elements, but also to whatever creatures may be lurking nearby. Not to mention the most dangerous monsters of all - other people.

This story is set on one such camping expedition, in a way. It began in early summer, after a few too many beers. Most of the best stories do. Four friends around a pub garden bench. Not close friends, it must be said, but the kind of friends with busy lives that meet up a couple of times a year to catch up on whatever news they may have that hasn't already been shared across social media. Daniel's online profile will tell you that he is in his early thirties, married, his wife has very recently given birth to their second child, and he is an estate agent. What his profile won't tell you is that he has a gambling habit which is in danger of costing him his home and his family. Steven's profile is as basic as possible, rarely updated, only adding a brief status every now and again so that those on his short friends list know he is still alive. His profile picture is of a skull, all other information has been left blank either through laziness, a desire for privacy, or some attempt at appearing mysterious. Steven is pleasant and will hold a lengthy conversation with you about almost anything - religion, politics, sexuality, films, books, and so on. He will show an apparently genuine interest in what you say, and what you tell him about yourself. But if you try to turn the conversation to his personal life then he will find an excuse to leave.

The other half of this seemingly mis-matched group are a couple. Incredibly average in appearance, you may notice them pass you by in a crowded room but would soon forget you had seen them. Average height, average build, not ugly but in no way attractive enough to warrant a second glance. The only thing that one would notice, if one were to look hard enough, was how happy, and how in love this young pair are. The constant need to be in contact, physically, with one another. The flirtatious looks passed between them, even as someone else may be talking. A deeply burning sexual desire that gives the impression they are dying to sneak off for some carnal pleasures at the first available opportunity. This is Martha and Noah. The trip was Noah's idea, and came across as a suggestion out of the blue, but Martha's lack of surprise suggested that the idea had been at least tossed around previously.

"Walk how far?!" Daniel asked, incredulously. "I take the car to the bloody shops."

"It's only twenty-five miles," Martha explained, backing up Noah's suggestion. "A couple of days stroll in the countryside at the most, and we can camp out for a night. The route starts just outside of town, following a trail which actually runs for one hundred miles. Some day we want to walk the whole thing." Noah smiled at Martha, nodding his head.

"Daniel won't do it," Steven interjected. "Not unless there is a five-star hotel along the way." The comment may have been made in jest, but it struck a nerve with Daniel.

"Funny fucker," Daniel retorted. "It's not that I don't want to, I mean it could be a laugh, I guess. But Holly wouldn't be happy about it. She's just had a baby and it was pushing my luck getting let out today. Disappearing overnight for a wander around in a field isn't going to make her happy."

"Well, I'm up for it," Steven announced. "When shall we go? I have a small tent and sleeping bag, will I need anything else?"

"Anyway, I don't have any camping stuff," Daniel pointed out. "I can't imagine you lovebirds will want me in with you two."

"There is room in my tent," Steven replied. "I've fit three people in it before."

"Fuck off! You only know three people and we're all here," Daniel said with a laugh. He was beginning to feel the pressure to join his friends on this ludicrous adventure but knew that it would only add to the tensions at home. *Maybe it would do us both some good to have a couple of days apart?* he pondered, aware that he was just making excuses to justify his intentions. "Fine," he continued, "but I have to let Holly know. I'll tell her by text before I get home, in case the Dutch courage wears off. When you wanna go?"

The next half hour was spent cross-checking suitable days with each other until an agreement was made. Saturday, in two weeks' time, meet back at the pub at midday for a pre-hike beverage or two. Daniel sent a text to his exhausted and depressed wife, who replied with one word - *Fine.* He understood it meant the complete opposite, but chose to ignore the fact, opting instead to grab some cheap flowers on his way home to soften the blow. Once Daniel had left, Martha and Noah made their excuses and headed back to their small flat, picking up a bottle of gin along the way, and heading inside for a drunken fumble on the sofa. Steven stayed for another drink, content in drinking alone, watching the other patrons as they talked and laughed. He felt invisible, but this did not upset him. It was as if he had a super power of sorts, and his mind drifted to fantasies of what he could do if were truly invisible. From shoplifting, to voyeuristic behaviour, to thoughts of bloodshed, Steven's mind wandered until he noticed the erection that had formed beneath the pub bench. *Fucking pervert,* he thought as he waited for the excitement to fade, enabling him to finally return to the damp-ridden bedsit that he called home.

Saturday, around midday, two weeks later.

"Didn't think you were going to make it," Martha said, greeting Daniel as he approached the bar. He was dressed in a perfectly pressed white shirt which was tucked into a pair of khaki shorts, and sporting what looked like brand-new hiking boots. He didn't smile, or respond to Martha, simply asking the bartender for a double Woodford Reserve on ice. Steven seized the moment.

"Holly not happy?" he asked, trying poorly to conceal a smirk. Daniel just looked at him, before turning back to his drink.

"We'll finish these up, then get going," Noah suggested, trying to lighten the mood. "He'll cheer up once we get going," he whispered to Martha.

"Either way, we'll have fun," she replied with a wink. The weather had been kind enough to allow for wearing shorts all round, and with only one night away there was not too much to bring. Daniel only had a small rucksack, having left the supply of any camping essentials to the others. Steven had, as promised, loaded himself up with a small tent, as well as a sleeping bag, and a large bottle of budget cider.

"Got everything you need?" Noah asked, doubtful that Daniel had put any thought into what would be needed.

"Clean underwear, toothbrush, half bottle of whiskey."

"Looks like we'll be sharing a sleeping bag tonight," Steven said with a wink. "I sleep naked, by the way."

"You wish," Daniel replied. "I'm sure I'll be warm enough without. What do you guys have? You look like you're going for a month!"

"Only the essentials; our small tent, sleeping bag each, snacks, torches, firelighters, first aid kit, clean clothes," Martha explained. She could see the look on the faces of the other two men as soon as she had said the word *snacks*. "No one else bring any food?"

"Sorry," Steven mumbled. "We'll go past a shop on the way and grab some bits. Maybe some hot-dogs to warm through if we're having a fire?"

"Sounds good, mate. And yes, definitely a fire. Wouldn't be camping without a fire and some ghost stories," Noah said.

"What are you, like twelve? You really think we'll be spooked by a campfire story?" Daniel asked, draining the last of his bourbon.

"We'll see," Martha said with a grin. "Now, can we get going?"

The group made their way, via a supermarket, to the start of the hillside trail. They were now a little more weighed down, having picked up a few beers, some ciders, more food, and a few bottles of water. But with nothing but green fields ahead, the therapeutic power of nature lifted everyone's mood, especially Daniel's.

"I didn't think I'd be saying it, but it is nice to get away, even if we are hiking through fields of cow shit."

"Told you it would be fun," Martha said, through a grin she had been wearing since leaving the pub. "And I'm glad you've cheered up a bit. Is Holly okay?" Daniel looked a little guilty.

"I guess so. We had a row; we're both so tired with the kids. She has gone to her mum's for a couple of days which is probably best for her, and I don't feel so bad for leaving her on her own."

"Well," Noah began, trying to be tactful, "as long as she has her mum to help out then I guess you just need to take the time to unwind. A break could be really helpful." Daniel didn't reply, simply nodding slowly as if he were thinking things over.

"So, I can assume one of you guys has a map, or some idea of where we go?" Steven asked, after they had been walking for a couple of hours.

"No map. But the trail is well signposted. It's split into four sections of approximately twenty-five miles each. This first quarter finishes at a pub called the Farmer's Thumb, which seemed like good place to end."

"And how do we get back? I'm not walking back again!"

"I've got a friend picking us up. Just need to call her when we get to the pub," Martha explained. "We've been at it for almost two and a half hours, which should be at least eight miles, maybe a little more. I'd say another hour and we'd be good to set up camp and crack open some beers." There was a murmur of agreement among the group, who were all keen to rest up, and get some drinks inside them. Their bottled water had almost gone already, leaving none for the following day, but no one had gone so far as to open any of the alcohol yet. Aside from a couple of pastries, the food also remained untouched, but stomachs rumbled at the thought of warm sausages.

"We have a few more hours of daylight before it'll be worth starting a fire, if you are even allowed to just have a fire in a field. Are we going to get a bollocking from some angry farmer?" Steven asked.

"I wouldn't worry about that. We are way too far from any other people to even be noticed. Out here, no-one will hear you scream," Noah answered, putting on a theatrical voice. "By the time we find a good spot, get the tents up, and find enough firewood, I'm sure it will be getting dark. That's when the real fun can begin."

"Oh you mean this hiking over hills in the middle of fucking nowhere isn't the fun part?" Daniel asked, looking to Noah expectantly for a genuine answer.

"This is good," Martha stated. "But later will be much more interesting."

Steven's Story

It was around an hour before dusk when the group reached a comparatively flat patch of grass, large enough to set up camp for the night, and reasonably well sheltered by a tree line to the south. No-one had spoken for some time, the reality of how far they were walking beginning to dampen their spirits, Daniel's in particular.

"Well, it's about fucking time," he grumbled when Noah suggested they stop.

"Good spot," Martha stated. "Flat, a bit sheltered, plus we should be able to find some firewood in those trees. Best get set up before it gets too dark." Steven slung his backpack to the ground and unzipped it to get to the tent he had brought. Using the excuse that he would get in the way, Daniel took a seat on the grass to watch Steven build their home for the night. The temperature was beginning to drop, and Daniel cursed himself for not bringing a sleeping bag, not that he would admit it to anyone. Instead, he pulled out the half bottle of whiskey and cracked the seal, hopeful that its golden warmth would see him through the night.

Martha and Noah completely emptied each of their bags, building a surprisingly large tent, and then furnishing it with a picnic blanket, roll mats, and sleeping bags. They positioned the entrance opposite to Steven's, allowing enough space for a fire to be constructed in the gap between. After less than an hour, the camp was built, and Daniel was making steady progress with his whiskey.

"How about you go and find some sticks for the fire, if you aren't too busy?" Martha suggested, her gaze fixed on Daniel. He looked as though he wanted to refuse but could not find the words to justify saying no, instead mumbling an 'okay' as he placed the bottle back into his bag.

"Can I take the torch?" he asked, noting how quickly the sun was fading and aware that within the trees it would be darker still. Noah passed it to him, clicking it on as he did so.

"Grab a load of small ones for the kindling, just make sure they are dry. And then we can all go and help with the larger pieces. Should be able to find enough to keep a fire going for a few hours."

Half an hour later and darkness was beginning to engulf the four friends, the crackling of the fire providing the only light. Each of their faces illuminated eerily by the flames as they licked upwards. The mood began to lift once the snacks had been consumed, and a dent had been made in the alcohol supply. There was a pause in the conversation, a moment of silence only punctuated by the cracking of the burning wood, and Martha took the opportunity to make a suggestion.

"Right, it wouldn't be a campfire without some stories. Who wants to go first?" The men all looked to one another, not wanting to be the first to speak.

"I'll go first," Steven offered. "As long as Daniel is going to join in after. What sort of story do you have in mind?"

"Something scary, with the four of us in it," Martha suggested.

"Fine," Daniel said. "It's not like there's much else to do. But I can't promise it'll be a good story."

"Okay Steven, let's see what you've got," Noah said. Steven cleared his throat, smirking a little as the ideas begin to form in his head.

"It was a dark and stormy night," he began, to the groans of everyone else. "Bear with me, please, lady and gentlemen. And no interruptions. It was a dark and stormy night, and four friends were lost, wandering in the wilderness."

"Sounds about right," Daniel interrupted. Steven ignored him.

"What should have been a simple country walk, travelling pub to pub, had resulted in a wrong turn somewhere along the way, and the group found themselves on the edge of a thick forest. The group had very little in the way of supplies, and tensions began to run high as the severity of their situation hit them. Nobody knew which way they should be walking, no-one could get a signal on their phone to call for help. They stopped to assess their predicament. To the south was the entrance to the forest, and it was impossible to see how far it went on for. To the north, a large hill rose up. The leader of the group, Noah, suggested climbing the hill in order to look for any sign of civilisation. Daniel, the least enthusiastic about being outdoors at all, sat down to sulk." At this point Steven was unable to hide a full grin, and Daniel leaned across and punched him on the leg.

"If I may continue?" Steven said, straightening up. "The group were in a perilous situation, everyone was certain of this. And Noah's suggestion of climbing the hill to the north seemed like a very sensible plan. Leaving Daniel to sulk and whine, the other three adventurers began the ascent. The steepness was such that they all had to virtually crawl up to the top, pulling tufts of grass to help themselves along. As soon as they reached the summit, the wind struck them with an icy force, causing them to visibly shake. All that could be seen in every direction was impenetrable darkness. 'We're going to die out here!' Martha wailed, teeth chattering, and tears forming in her eyes. 'Wait! What's that? Is that a house?'. Steven had spotted a faint light in the distance, and what could well be smoke billowing from a chimney. 'It's hard to tell from here,' Noah replied. 'But it's as good a plan as any. Could be a farm house, and we may be able to call for help from there.'

The trio half-climbed, half-slid back down the hill to find Daniel still rooted to the spot. Thankful to be out of the wind, and to have some hope that they would survive this disastrous expedition, they explained the plan to Daniel. 'Through the forest?' he asked incredulously. 'You're mad, there could be anything living in there.'

'Fine, stay here then. But we're going to that house and getting help,' Steven announced, heading for the entrance to the woodland. Daniel rose with a grunt. 'It didn't look all that far, we just need to keep our path straight.' Four flashlight apps were turned on, on four mobile phones, and the beams focused on the ground before them. Leaves and branches cracked as the four began their voyage through the forest, crushing the brittle sticks as they went. The group continued in silence, eyes transfixed on each step they took. Seemingly out of nowhere, a huge oak to their right shook, expelling a small flock of birds which had been hiding within its branches. The sound of their wings flapping filled the night air, someone in the group let out a squeal, and everyone felt their hearts racing.

'Jesus Christ!' Noah exclaimed, with a nervous laugh. 'That scared the shit out of me!' The group trudged onward, trying to brace themselves for another flurry of activity in the treetops.

'I need a piss,' Daniel announced from the back of the line. 'Wait up.' Stopping where he stood, Daniel unzipped and began watering the foliage with his whiskey tainted scent. The rest of the group had stopped walking, in order to not get out of sight of Daniel, but kept their eyes facing forward and waited for the sound of Daniel's spray to cease. It came to a stop suddenly but was not followed by the sound of a zipper being pulled back up, or the sound of cracking twigs as he re-joined the group. The next sound that the group heard was a brief whizzing noise, followed by a thud. Noah, Martha, and Steven looked at one another, before shining their lights back in the direction of the sound. Daniel's phone was on the ground, its light shining towards the forest canopy.

'Daniel?' Martha called. Silence. 'Stop fucking about.' Steven began to take a few steps towards the discarded phone, scanning the area with his own when his light found its target. Steven wanted to scream, but the sound was beaten by a rush of vomit spattering from his mouth. Before the others could query Steven's reaction, they too saw what lie before them. Daniel was lying on the forest floor. Martha ran her light from Daniel's shoes, up his legs, spotted his shrivelled manhood still poking out from the zipper, and that is where

Daniel stopped. A mess of gore protruded from his waist line, innards soiling the leafy floor, a mixture of stomach contents and shit intermingled, and Steven vomited again.

'Where's the rest of him?' Martha asked. It was a reasonable question, along with 'What the fuck could have done this?' and 'Why the hell aren't we running yet?'. Noah reached down to retrieve Daniel's phone, proceeding to shine two lights around, whilst cautious not to step into the mess that Daniel had been reduced to. There was no sign of the top half of their friend anywhere around, and it was not until Martha felt a warm drip land on her cheek, causing her to look up, that they found him. Sprawled across two branches, a good twenty feet above them, blood dripping from his waistline, was Daniel.

'How the fuck did he get up there?' Steven demanded, turning to leave. 'We need to get out of here.' Martha cast her light over the top half of Daniel one more time, wanting to see his face before they made their escape. As the brightness of the light landed on the wounded man's face, his eyes squinted, just a little.

'Oh my God! He's still alive,' Martha shrieked. 'Look!' The three directed their light at the soon-to-be corpse of their friend and, as horrifying as it was, saw him squint and let out a gargled cough. 'We need to get him down!' Martha continued. Steven and Noah looked at one another.

'Listen, I know that we shouldn't just leave him up there, but there is no way of getting him down ourselves. And you know he isn't going to make it.' Although Martha understood perfectly well what she was being told, it still felt wrong to leave him there like that.

'Then we wait with him until...well, you know.'

'I really don't think hanging around here is a good move. It's shit what happened to Daniel, but I don't fancy getting hacked into pieces myself. We need to move. Now.' Steven was right, the others knew it, and Noah had no choice but to almost drag Martha onward into the woods. Someone, or something, was in there with them. Something deadly, something silent, and something with murderous intentions.

The trio had picked up the pace, with no concern about how much noise they made as they cracked their way through the undergrowth. The only plan was to reach the house on the other side of the woods, and the safety that it would bring. All eyes were transfixed on the floor before them, in small patches that their lights illuminated. Noah followed in Steven's footsteps, and Martha in Noah's. They were close enough to one another to hear the heavy breathing of each other, brought on by a mix of fear and the rapid pace they tried to maintain. The air was pierced with a loud thud, and Steven fell backwards to the ground, causing Noah and Martha to collide with him and end up sprawled across one another.

Cautiously Noah shone his light across Steven's body, expecting to find he had met the same fate as Daniel. Murmurs from Steven's mouth suggested otherwise. Across his forehead a large, red bump was quickly forming. Martha let slip a small laugh. Noah, certain this situation was not an amusing one, threw her a glance, before following the beam of light emanating from Martha's phone.

'You walked straight into that branch," she said, relieved that that was all that had happened.

'Well, it hurts like a bastard!' Steven replied, trying to stand.

'I'm sure you'll live. Now let's get...' Martha's attempt to hurry them along was cut short by a familiar whizzing sound. Noah and Steven stared at her as her eyes bulged and she seemed to be pleading with them. As her lips attempted to move, fresh crimson bubbles appeared in her mouth and a red drool soaked her chin. The men looked on in horror as a gruesome line, dark and wet, appeared horizontally beneath Martha's breasts. Noah reached for her a little too late, as the top half of her body slid away from the rest of her, and her legs dropped to the ground. This time it was Noah's turn to vomit, as the viscera formed a pool among the leaves and the faint light in Martha's eyes went out.

Steven turned to run, but Noah would not. Witnessing the murder of his friend was one thing, but for his lover to meet the same fate was more than he could take. They were being hunted in this forest, and the only rational explanation that Noah could come up with was that their attacker was human, and well-trained. There was no guessing at *why* this was happening, and Noah knew inside that he stood little chance of taking on this foe, but his will to live was rapidly dwindling.

'If I'm going to die, and I'm pretty sure we're all fucked, then I'm taking this bastard with me.' Steven was not so sure.

'You do what you've got to do. I'm getting to that house and calling the police. This isn't some bar fight; whoever is doing this is a fucking psychopath.' With that, he tuned on his heels and disappeared further into the trees. Noah screamed into the blackness, daring their enemy to show himself. A breeze disturbed the leaves in the trees, but no other sound could be heard. Whoever was hunting them clearly knew their way around these woods and was able to take out Martha with them standing only a few feet away. No-one had heard anyone approach. Daniel wasn't a small man; to have managed to get half of him that high into the tree would have taken impressive strength. Or something beyond what could be predicted.

Noah knew he had little choice but to follow in the same direction as Steven. He hated to admit it, but he would be no match against this unseen force, and surely the police would be the best option. It was barely possible to tell which way Steven had travelled, but there were small signs if one looked closely enough; a few bent branches, faint footprints in the mud. All Noah could do was to keep a steady pace and pray that he did not hear that whizzing sound again, knowing all too well that if he did then it would be too late.

Steven burst through the tree line on the other side of the forest, panting heavily. He looked around to see the cottage they had spotted was another five hundred metres or so from where he stood. Despite his exhaustion, the chance of salvation spurred him on, providing him with enough energy to sprint to the house. Fists clenched, he hammered on the front door continuously until he saw a light come on inside.

'Help!' he screamed. The door opened a little, just the width of the security chain, and he was greeted by a man in his late sixties. If there was ever a stereotypical image of a farmer who had been awoken from his sleep then this was it; striped pyjamas covered a round physique, flat cap placed on an almost hairless scalp.

'What's going on?' the farmer asked, his eyes darting around behind Steven as though afraid of what may be out there.

'My friends,' Steven managed to say between breaths. 'Dead. Someone in the woods, killed them.' Still, the farmer kept looking over Steven's shoulder, scanning the tree line in the distance. Cautiously, the farmer unchained the door.

'You'd better come in then, and we can call the police.' The farmer showed Steven through to a quaint living room and motioned for him to take a seat. 'How many of your friends were out there?' he asked.

'There were four of us,' Steven began, tears forming in his eyes. 'We were out hiking and got lost. Two of them are dead for sure, sliced in half by someone, or something. Noah could still be alive, but I doubt it. He went to look for whoever was out there.'

'You just stay put, son,' the farmer said. 'I'll go fetch the phone and the police can come and deal with this mess. Can I get you a glass of water? Or something stronger?' Steven looked at his hands, watching them tremble.

'A Scotch would be great, if you have any?'

'Coming right up. You rest for a moment, and we'll have this all sorted before long.'

A few moments later the farmer returned with two tumblers filled with whiskey, the ice cubes clattering against the glasses as he passed one to Steven.

'And the phone?' Steven asked.

'I just called them, told them what you told me. I'll be honest son, they sounded skeptical, but will be sending someone out as soon as they can. We're a bit cut off out here so could be an hour or so.' Steven went to say something but thought better of it, deciding there was little he could say to hurry things along. He drained the Scotch in a matter of a few minutes and was furnished with a second almost immediately.

'This'll take the edge off,' the farmer said as he handed over a second, larger glass. Three mouthfuls into the drink, and Steven's eyes began to close. *Exhaustion?* Steven wondered as he felt himself starting to doze, but this felt different. His mind felt alert, but his body seemed to be shutting down. He was too weak to raise his arms, and he heard his glass slip from his hand and strike the wooden floor.

'That's right, you just rest,' Steven heard, unable to reply. As he tried to make sense of the new predicament he now found himself in, Steven's thoughts were interrupted by a banging at the door of the cottage. *The police,* he thought. This thought did not linger long once he heard the farmer's greeting.

'What the bloody hell have you two been up to out there? And what in God's name is that?' Steven heard the shuffling of feet, as the visitors made their way into the living room. 'You,' the farmer continued, 'are bloody lucky that this one came here.' It didn't take long for

Steven to make the connection between the farmer and whoever had been in the woods, and the realisation that the police were not on their way hit him hard. It took an enormous amount of strength to force one eye open, but Steven simply had to see who was there.

Steven's one open eye was faced by another, mere inches from his. Despite the vacant look in it, there was also a familiarity in that brown sphere. As his eye searched the peripheral of his limited view, he could make out the forehead and the matted, dark hair, that was unmistakably Noah's. For the briefest moment, Steven thought that Noah was somehow involved in the horror of the last few hours. That was until he saw the mud-covered hand, fingers weaved through Noah's hair, casually holding Steven's friend's head at waist height. Only his head. If Steven had not been paralysed by whatever was slipped into the Scotch, he would, undoubtedly, have screamed. His one good eye, desperate to seek answers, flitted across as much of the room as possible without moving his head. The voices were clear; the farmer reprimanding at least two assailants as if they were simply naughty children.

'But we didn't have a choice. The chance to practice is pretty rare,' one of them said. The voice sounded young, but what surprised Steven more than this was the fact that the voice also sounded female.

'You said we need to be ready, remember? That when they come to take our land, we must defend it. I thought that was the point of all this training Dad?' the other one reasoned. *Dad?* Steven thought. *Two farmer's daughters have done all this? Training? What are they, fucking ninjas?*

'You girls have gone too far, and you leave me no choice but to confiscate your weapons.' This was met with petulant groans from the psychotic females. 'For two weeks,' the farmer continued. Steven watched as several samurai swords were dropped to the ground, along with Noah's head. 'And you need to go back out there and clear up your mess!'

'We can't if we're grounded,' one of them replied, which was met with a slap from their father.

'Dad?' the other girl said, a little hesitantly. The farmer looked at her, expecting more bad news. 'We used a cable to hoist one of them into a tree. Thought it'd be a good warning. Should we take it down? It's awfully high.' There was a sigh from the farmer.

'Go to your rooms, and we'll clear up tomorrow. You better hope no-one comes by before then. You'll have to strip them and bury the clothes and belongings; the animals will take care of the rest.'

'What about this one?' Steven heard, knowing his fate was sealed.

'We'll hang on to him for now. Maybe if you have someone here to practice on then you'll stop going out looking for trouble. Grab some cable ties and stick him in the basement.'

"So," Daniel began. "I get chopped up almost immediately and you get to live with a couple of sexy ninjas?"

"I never said they were sexy," Steven replied. "But now you've said it, maybe I end up living there as their sex slave. Could be worse I suppose."

"Probably better than your stinky bedsit," Daniel said. "So, what did you guys think of Steven's story?"

"I really enjoyed it," Martha stated with a smile. "Nice and gruesome, which I like, and it was creepy enough." Noah nodded in agreement.

"Before we hear another one, the fire will need topping up. Who fancies going into the woods for some more sticks?" Noah asked with a smirk.

"Fuck that," Daniel said, crossing his arms.

"Ooh, did my story frighten you?" Steven teased, as he stood. "Don't worry, big man, I'll go. But I want to hear your story next."

"I don't know any stories," Daniel mumbled. "But fine, just give me a theme or something."

"Aliens!" Martha blurted out. "Sorry, first thing that I thought of. Just not set in the woods this time please, or we'll never sleep! And starring the four of us again, I liked that."

Daniel spent the next twenty minutes sipping at his whiskey, deep in thought about what he would say, whilst Steven went back and forth into the trees in search of firewood. Once the flames had reached a more desirable level, and a stockpile had been placed nearby, the four were ready to hear Daniel's attempt at a tale about aliens. He shifted uncomfortably in his chair; despite the whiskey he still did not have the confidence to begin. Then, seemingly from out of nowhere, he looked as though he had an idea of where the story would go. Taking one long swig, he cleared his throat and prepared to begin.

"Okay guys, I don't have a title for this masterpiece yet, but here goes. Once upon a time..." Martha giggled, Steven groaned, and Noah waited, stone-faced, listening intently.

Daniel's Story

"Once upon a time..." Daniel repeated. The others sat in silence, basking in the warmth of the flames, sipping at their drinks. "...four friends had, for some unknown reason, decided to take a hike in the wilderness. Our hero, Daniel, led the motley crew across peaks and valleys. He was an athletic man; muscular, Hollywood-handsome, and a keen adventurer." Again, Martha laughed, as Steven simply rolled his eyes and resisted the urge to make any derogatory comments. Daniel was smirking, beginning to enjoy his moment in the spotlight. "Following their intrepid leader were Steven, Martha, and Noah. Steven looked up to Daniel, virtually worshipping the ground upon which he trod, just happy to have been allowed to join in on the adventure. Martha and Noah were a couple, and highly experienced in orienteering. As happy as their relationship seemed, Daniel would catch the occasional glance from Martha; a look of longing in her beautiful eyes."

"Careful," Noah said, his face looking serious. There was an awkward moment of silence before Daniel spoke again.

"It's just a story, mate. But fine, okay. Where was I?"

"You were talking about my beautiful eyes," Martha said. Noah shot her an unimpressed glance.

"Yes, well, anyway. Daniel led his team of followers across the wilderness, relishing in the beauty of summer in the English countryside, as they searched for the perfect spot to set up camp that evening. While the others gathered firewood, Daniel set about putting up tents, and ensuring that everyone would be comfortable and well looked after."

"Have you ever even put a tent up?" Steven asked, getting a little irritated by Daniel's self-appreciation.

"It's just a story, like I said. You guys are so sensitive! The evening passed like so many before; the team ate, drank a little too much, and discussed the adventurous plans they had for the future. It was a clear night, yet still warm at the peak of summer. The stars could be seen clearly, glistening against the backdrop of a blueish-black sky. Daniel tilted his head back to take a sip of twenty-five-year-old Scotch, and that is when he saw it. At first, he thought it was a shooting star. 'Did you guys see that?' he asked. The others only looked at him quizzically. 'See what?' Noah replied. 'It looked like a shooting star,' Daniel told him. The group all looked heavenward, hoping to catch sight of another one, or perhaps it was the start of a meteor shower. They did not have to wait long. Moments later, another light whizzed overhead, then another, followed by several more. 'Well, that was cool,' Steven declared, just as the silence of the evening was interrupted by a huge crash to the south. Everyone's gaze shifted in the direction of the sound, just in time to see a large cloud of dust rise from the bottom of a field, no more than a few hundred yards away.

'Meteorite?' Martha asked, excitedly. The group scrambled out of their camping chairs, running to the crash site with torches in hand. The crater was sizable, a good six feet in diameter, but there was no sign of any extra-terrestrial rock. 'I don't see anything,' Steven said. 'But can you feel the heat coming from the hole? Maybe it burned up on the way through.' It was a solid theory, and disappointment was etched on Martha's face.

'The top layer just looks like dust; perhaps whatever it was has penetrated the top soil?' Noah suggested, squatting down to brush the dry earth away. He jumped back with a screech as soon as his hand met the soil. 'Fuck! It's too hot.' Noah looked at his hand under the torchlight, which had reddened and was already starting to blister. Cautiously, Daniel began to scrape some of the dusty soil away with his hiking boots. The boots seemed to withstand the heat well enough, but he could feel the temperature rise inside of them. A few inches of dirt removed, Daniel's boot hit something solid.

'There is something in there,' he said, kicking more enthusiastically at the surrounding earth. The others shone their lights into the crater, expecting to find a piece of space rock. As Daniel uncovered the item, it took them all by surprise. A rock it may have been, but to be shaped in a perfect sphere seemed incredibly unlikely - alien even. 'What the fucking hell is that thing?' Steven asked, taking a step back. Daniel looked serious.

'I don't know, but we need to get it out of there and up to the camp.'

'Is that a good idea?' Steven asked, clearly afraid of the orb. There was something unsettling about it, aside from its arrival from space. The colouring was unlike anything the group had seen before - a deep green colour which looked as though it had been polished to a perfect shine. It looked solid, and not, to Steven's relief, like an egg.

'We can't just leave it here,' Martha said. She was transfixed by the orb, unable to take her eyes off the thing, looking at it as though she had to have it. Her face reminded Daniel of Gollum, and his desire for The Ring.

'Right,' Noah interrupted, 'but it could still be too hot to touch, and I don't fancy burning my hands again.'

'Then we wait,' Martha insisted. 'Or we get some water to put on it.'

'I think we should just cover it back up,' Steven said, sounding nervous. 'There's something fucking wrong with that thing.'

'Don't be such a pussy,' Daniel retorted. 'If you want to get away from it then go and get a jug of water and we'll see how hot this thing is.' Reluctantly, Steven made his way back to the campsite and fetched a large water carrier. He didn't hurry himself, still certain that whatever that orb was, it should be left well alone.

'You took your time,' Daniel scolded, as Steven reappeared. Daniel only received a grunt in reply. After unscrewing the lid to the ten-litre container, Daniel lifted it above the hole and slowly began pouring it over the orb. Nothing. No hiss of steam, no reaction of any kind. Hesitantly, Daniel moved a hand closer to it. 'I can't feel any heat coming from it now,' he said. Everyone looked on in silence. Daniel placed a hand on the deep green surface. 'Weird,' he whispered. 'It's not hot, or cold particularly.' Feeling as though it was safe to touch, Daniel used both hands to surround the orb, pulling it from the ground. Despite only being around six inches in diameter, the thing must have weighed a good thirty pounds. 'But it's fucking heavy!' Daniel declared. It took all his strength to lift it out of the hole and carry it back up to the camp.

As mysterious as the events of the evening had been, there was little they could do to investigate the orb. It sat on a patch of dirt beside the fire, as the group continued with their drinks well into the night. The three men chatted, as though this were any other evening; even Steven seemed to have relaxed a little by this point. It was just Martha that kept staring at the orb, almost willing it to do something.

Daniel and Steven were sharing a tent, and both headed inside soon after two in the morning. Noah took this as his cue and touched Martha's arm. As soon as his flesh touched hers, his hand jerked back automatically. She was cold. Not cold to the touch just because she had been sat in a field in the middle of the night, but cold as if she had been pulled from an icy lake or rescued from being locked in a walk-in freezer.

'Martha?' Noah whispered. Her gaze was still fixed on the orb. 'Martha baby, you're freezing. Let's get you into the tent.' She did not respond, just continued to stare. Noah stood from his chair, before crouching down in front of her. Her eyes remained focused, but not on Noah. 'Honey, you're scaring me here. What are you doing?' Still nothing. Noah, frustrated, waved his hands in front of Martha's face, obscuring her view of the orb. This time she looked at him, her eyes void of recognition, before swinging her arm and striking him across the side of his head. Noah fell from his crouching position, on to his side. 'What the fuck?' he exclaimed, trying to stand. 'That bloody thing needs to go, you're acting like a maniac!' Grabbing the picnic blanket, which had been positioned at the entrance to Daniel and Steven's tent, Noah threw it over the orb to break Martha's fixated glare. No sooner had the blanket landed, cutting off Martha's line of sight, and she was up and out of her chair.

The wine bottle which had sat empty on the floor beside her was now in her hand, as she swung ferociously for Noah. He took a couple of steps backwards, yelling for the others. Before he knew what was happening, Noah's foot caught in a rabbit hole, turning the ankle in a way it was not supposed to turn. His foot gave out, sending him toppling into the fire with a scream. Daniel and Steven appeared from their tent to see Noah face down in the camp fire, being held in place by Martha. The sight took too long to process, as the two men stared at the burned remains of their friend, face melted beyond recognition.

As if nothing had happened, Martha stepped out of the fire, unmarked by its heat, removed the picnic blanket from the orb, and resumed her position on the chair. She did not appear to register the presence of the other two men, who simply stared in stunned silence.

'What do we do?' Steven whispered. Daniel was already backing into the tent, hands trembling as he fumbled for his phone.

'Shit! Battery is dead. Where's yours?' Steven pointed to his side of the tent.

'In the sleeping bag. I turned to off to save battery. Should be working,' he explained, still keeping his voice low. Daniel hit the power button on the side of the handset, and the screen illuminated blue with the manufacturer's logo. Both men jumped as the start-up jingle blared from the phone, shattering the silence they were trying to maintain. Steven's head immediately turned to where Martha had been sitting, finding only an empty chair. Turning fully around he scanned the immediate area for any sign of movement, seeing nothing. 'She's gone,' Steven said. 'And so is that creepy bowling ball!'

Daniel exited the tent, verifying what he had been told. 'She can't get far with it, it weighs a ton. We should stay here and wait for the police. I'm not hunting around in the dark for her.' He keyed the number into the phone, eyes searching in the distance for signs of Martha. Steven could hear the phone ring, once, twice, then a whizzing sound, followed by a warm splatter across his face. His hands instinctively rose to wipe his eyes, and he looked down at his blood-soaked fingers. It took a fraction of a second to realise that this wasn't his blood.

Across from the fire stood Martha, hands outstretched with her palms facing where Daniel had been standing. Steven was shaking, entirely due to fear, and felt a warm trickle down the inside leg of lounge pants. Preparing himself for the worst, he turned to look through the entrance to the tent. The orb was inside the tent, its polished, deep green colour now matted with blood, hair, and other gruesome additions. Daniel's body was slumped on its back, having been thrown backwards a few feet.

Steven realised that the whizzing sound had been the orb passing him, at a speed impossible for its weight. Its path had taken it from Martha's hands to its place in the tent, via Daniel's ribcage. A huge hole had ripped through Daniel, exposing ribs which jutted out of the cavity in all directions, and Steven felt the bile rise within him.

'What now?' he yelled across the fire to Martha. 'What happens now?' Martha walked directly towards Steven, through the fire, and stood before him.

'The orb is mine,' she said, her voice monotone, almost robotic.

'I didn't fucking want it anyway,' Steven replied. 'I don't want to die.' He was trying his hardest not to cry, but it was all becoming too much.

'You do not have to die,' Martha replied. 'You can join us.'

'Join you? Who? What the hell are you talking about?'

'It's almost time,' Martha said, cryptically, and sat herself inside Steven's tent, one hand lovingly stroking the orb. Steven wanted to run. More than anything, he wanted to be as far away from this place as possible, as far away from that thing. He had no doubt, however, that if he tried then he would meet the same fate as Daniel, so he slumped into a chair in his piss-soaked lounge pants and cracked open the last can of ale.

The ale lasted Steven almost half an hour, as he stared through watery, bloodshot eyes at Noah's body, continuing the burn in front of him. His thoughts of helplessness and his own impending demise where shattered by a rumble not dissimilar to thunder. From within his tent, a light flashed, so bright that his eyes closed of their own accord. Once he was able to reopen his eyes and fix his focus on the entrance to his tent, he felt his bladder weaken once more. Standing just outside of the tent stood Martha. The orb was in her hands, but no longer spherical. Each hand held a half of the orb, now glowing with a deep green light. Martha herself seemed to be emitting that same ghostly shade of light, her eyes now a deep jade in colour.

'Come to me,' she demanded, in a voice that was certainly not her own. Steven did as he was commanded, his legs appearing to obey regardless of what his brain told them to do. As he approached, Martha held out one of the half-orbs for him to take. He felt a loss of control, as though he were a puppet, despite his mind attempting to fight against it. He saw his own arms rise and take the offered piece of the orb. Looking at the exposed inner part of the sphere, Steven saw what looked like a ring. It was as black as could be, blacker than anything of this earth, he was sure. Etched around the surface of the ring, in that deep green colour, seemed to be an inscription of some kind, but not in any language he could possibly recognise.

'We are your servants,' Martha shouted, taking the ring from her piece of the orb, and placing it on Steven's finger. No sooner had she done so, and Steven felt a power surge through him. He felt stronger, almost indestructible. His mind cleared, the monumental fear that he had felt had completely dissipated, and he now knew his mission. Taking the ring from his sphere, he placed it on Martha's hand, uniting them.

Martha led Steven into the tent, ignoring the gruesome remains of Daniel, and undressed."

"Hang on a minute," Noah interrupted. "You can skip the details."

"Yeah, I don't really want to hear what you can imagine me doing, thanks," Martha said, backing up Noah's request. Daniel looked a little disappointed.

"Fine," he continued. "They undressed, did some weird alien sex stuff, and drifted off to sleep. That okay?"

"Hmm, carry on," Noah replied.

"It was light when Martha awoke, naked, and in a tent which was not her own. 'Noah?' she asked, feeling the warmth of a man holding her from behind. Steven stirred. Martha screamed. 'Steven! What the fuck?' Steven looked just as puzzled, and a little afraid of what had happened.

'How much did we drink last night?' he asked, sitting up and placing a hand over his genitals. There was a stench permeating the tent, and Steven looked across the groundsheet to see the bloody mess that had previously been Daniel. 'Holy shit!' Martha looked in the same direction, jumping up from where she lay. She quickly grabbed some clothes from the pile she had discarded the night before and ran from the tent to find Noah. Steven was just pulling on some shorts when he heard the scream, followed by loud sobbing, and Martha wailing Noah's name.

'Fuck!' Steven cursed. 'Do you remember anything?' Martha simply shook her head, continuing to cry. 'We need to call someone,' Steven said, searching around for a phone to use. There was no sign of his, and Daniel's appeared to have a dead battery. Steven moved purposefully to the other tent and as he reached into Noah's bag to retrieve a phone from there, he spotted something out of place. Perhaps not as out of place as his two dead friends, but unsettling nonetheless. 'Martha?' he called from the entrance of the tent. She turned her head. 'Why am I wearing some weird wedding ring?'

Martha looked at her own hands, now soaked with tears. Sure enough, she also wore a black wedding band, inscribed with an unknowable green script. 'We need to get out of here. Right now,' she declared. 'I don't think saying we can't remember is going to be good enough.' Her face showed determination through the shock, as though running away would clear her name. Steven could offer no better solution, opting to help get a bag of essentials together and leave the grisly scene behind.

Martha and Steven walked in silence through the fields, avoiding anywhere in which people might be found, and sleeping under the stars for weeks on end. They hardly spoke during this time and were not intimate with one another again. They felt as though they were wandering without purpose, their only aim to distance themselves from the horrors of that night. It wouldn't be much longer before Martha notices the deep green lines forming across her abdomen and, soon after that, the feeling of a life growing inside of her. A life not of this world."

No-one spoke for a few moments, so Daniel broke the silence.

"Well, what did you think?"

"I really liked it," Steven said, a little sheepishly.

"That's just because you got to bang me," Martha said, enjoying being the only female in the group. "Don't worry, I liked it too. Probably because I ended up as a bad-ass alien queen or something."

"And you Noah, what did you think?" Daniel asked. He had resisted detailing the sex scene in his story, but it was evident that Noah had felt uncomfortable, even if it was just a story.

"I actually thought it was pretty good. My favourite part was when you got a space orb through the chest." Noah didn't laugh, or even give any hint of humour as he said this. He simply fixed Daniel with a stare which was far from friendly.

"Okay," Daniel mumbled slowly. "So, who's next?" Noah and Martha looked at each other.

"I'd like to go last, if you don't mind?" Martha said. Noah didn't reply. "We just need a theme, or do you already have an idea?" Noah paused, looking towards the tree line.

"I think," he began, "that a traditional ghost story would be quite fitting. Just give me a few minutes to have a think."

"Good idea," Steven said. "I need a piss anyway." The group took the opportunity to refresh their drinks, open a few large bags of crisps and nuts, and go for toilet breaks. Noah added a few of the larger logs to the fire and prepared to begin.

"Ready?" he asked.

"Ready," the others replied in unison.

"Then I will begin. Oh, hang on." Noah felt around under his chair for the torch, clicked it on, and shone it upwards from beneath his chin. "That's better," he said with a smile at last. "Now I will begin."

Noah's Story

"The storm made landfall with little warning. The heat of the summer's day had been welcome; a perfect day for the camping trip which had been planned months in advance. A long weekend in the great outdoors, escaping from the tedium of everyday life, had been much needed for the group. The foursome had chosen a route along the coast, with no particular finishing point in mind; they would simply walk, and camp, for four days before finding public transport to take them home. It had been overcast on Friday when they left, but sufficiently warm to make the first part of the adventure pleasant enough. The first night's camping had gone well, and they had awoken to glorious sunshine and clear skies.

Towards the end of the second day, around twelve miles from their starting point, the weather took a turn. To their left, they were able to see nothing but green and brown fields; not another person in sight. To their right, sprawled out as far as the eye could see, was the English Channel. The stillness of the air surrounding them was in stark contrast to the weather on the horizon; clouds almost black in colour had formed, sheets of rain could be made out in the distance, and the low rumble of thunder carried through the air.

'I hope that stays out to sea,' Noah said, stopping to look at the impending storm.

Steven looked up from his phone, his face looking unimpressed.

'It's supposed to hit later, but there isn't a lot we can do about it. Just don't set the tents up too close to the cliff edge; it could be a windy night. How much farther shall we go before setting up?'

'I think there is a flatter area past the next couple of cliff tops,' Martha explained. 'It'll be a little more sheltered there.' The group moved onward, all feeling nervous about the storm, fearful that the night could be a challenge. It took the group less than twenty minutes to reach the area that Martha had described, but they could feel the patter of rain beginning to fall before they could even begin to unpack.

'I really don't want to be setting up in the rain,' Steven grumbled. 'Everything will be wet before we even get into the tents. And I'm pretty sure mine leaks.'

'Well,' Daniel began, scanning their surroundings, 'it's either we set up quickly and hope for the best, or we sleep in there.' He nodded towards what looked like a pill box, half buried into the slope of the hill to their left.

'I'll take my chances in the tent,' Martha stated with some certainty. 'Those things stink of piss and stale beer. It's probably full of discarded condoms and needles.'

'Maybe, but what if it isn't? Worth a quick look. We might be able to shelter in there just long enough for the storm to pass,' Noah suggested, flicking on a torch and walking away from the group. The wind had picked up and had brought with it a chill from the ocean. Martha, Daniel, and Steven stayed where they were, waiting for Noah to return.

Noah flashed the torch through the slots in the pill box, piercing the darkness. From this limited view, he could only see the other walls, and not the floor of the small room. The group watched as Noah disappeared around one side, in search of the entrance. A moment later they could see torchlight moving about inside briefly, before Noah made his return to the group. The three looked at him expectantly.

'Right, there are some crisp packets, a couple of empty vodka bottles, and a few little black bags which probably contain dog shit that someone has posted through the slots. That said, it doesn't really smell in there, and it's dry. I'm happy to bag up the rubbish and set out sleeping bags inside.'

'Is there room for all of us?' Daniel asked, worried that it would be even more cramped than the two-man tent he was sharing with Steven.

'It's bigger than the tents combined, so should be quite comfy. But we need to get in there now, before we are all soaked through.'

It did not take the group long to gather the rubbish to one side and set out a couple of picnic blankets to sit on. The inside of the pill box was completely dry, as Noah had said, but was also very nearly pitch black. So as not to run down all their torches, they kept them off for as long as possible, allowing their eyes to adjust to the darkness as well as possible. The group spent some time chatting, listening to the wind howl outside as the rain pelted down, and felt rather snug in their new shelter. Daniel fell asleep before the others, with Steven nodding off soon after. The two men had positioned their sleeping bags at the end farthest from the entrance, and now Noah was glad of that fact.

'I need a piss,' he told Martha, kissing her on the cheek as he rose.

'Me too, actually. Think I'd rather have someone with me.' Noah offered his hand and the pair exited the pill box, armed only with their torches. The area was remote enough for no-one to be around, especially so late at night, and with Daniel and Steven snoring there was little reason to be prudish. Noah stood facing away from the wind, rain soaking his back, and relieved himself against the outside wall of the pill box. Martha had waited for him to finish before requesting that he provide some shelter for her, which he did by standing between her and the beating rain.

'This weather is horrific,' Noah mumbled, watching Martha pull her jeans back up.

'I kinda like it,' she replied. 'It's fun.' Noah felt Martha pull him close, before kissing him deeply. Her hands began to wander across the front of his jeans, and he pushed her against the wall of the pill box.

'Here?' Noah asked, trying to ignore the cold water which had found its way down the back of his shirt.

'Yes please,' Martha replied, fumbling with the buttons on Noah's jeans.

A short while later, the pair returned the relative comfort of the pill box."

"I bet it was a *very* short while later," Daniel piped up, amused by his own comment. Noah didn't reply, but Martha gave him a patronising tap on the arm.

"Don't listen to Daniel, you do very well darling."

"Can I continue?" Noah asked, when he was satisfied everyone had stopped laughing at him. "Before I lose my train of thought."

"Apologies," Daniel said sarcastically. "Please do carry on."

"Noah and Martha, now tired and satisfied from their activities, climbed into their sleeping bags finally ready to call it a night, a little after 1am. 'Wake up!' came a voice, rousing Noah from his sleep. 'For fuck's sake, will you guys wake up!'. Noah slowly opened his eyes, only to shut them again as a torch was shone in his face.

'Jesus!' he muttered.

'Not Jesus, Steven,' Steven said. 'I need a piss really badly, but I can't find the fucking way out!'

'Oh, for God's sake.' Noah fumbled beside his sleeping bag to locate his torch and clicked it on. 'It's over...' Noah paused before he spoke again. 'Hang on,' he said, struggling to get out of his sleeping bag.

'I know where it *was*,' Steven retorted. 'I looked all the way around, but it isn't there now.'

'Don't be so bloody ridiculous!' Noah said, clearly agitated. 'An open doorway doesn't disappear. We must have just moved about in our sleep.' But sure enough, after inspecting every inch of all four walls, there was no doorway. The slits were still as before, thankfully allowing enough air to circulate within the pill box, but the entrance they had used was no longer there. Noah's first thought was that he was dreaming, but Steven convinced him that this was not the case. Noah's second thought was that someone had filled it in while they slept. This was, of course, a terrifying thought, but there was no sign that this could have happened; each part of the wall was identical, and certainly appeared to have been made all at one time.

'We're trapped in here!' Noah stated, unsure of whether to believe his own words.

'Not exactly,' Steven replied. 'There is the other door, behind you.' Noah spun around and was greeted by a wooden door fitted into the wall, solid looking, with a round, brass handle.

'What the fuck? We just looked all the way around. That wasn't there, was it?'

'I don't think so,' Steven replied. 'I don't know. I'm feeling really muddled, and I really do have to piss.'

'Go in the corner then,' Noah suggested, gently shaking Martha's shoulder. 'Honey, wake up.' She murmured a little, but her eyes remained closed. 'I really need you to wake up.' A shout from across the room finally caused Martha to open her eyes. Noah shone his torch to the other side, finding Daniel sat up and glaring at Steven.

'Fucking prick just pissed on me!' Daniel shouted, pulling himself up.

'It was just a bit of splash back from the wall, nothing I could do about it. Don't go getting all worked up and pretend you didn't like it.' Daniel stood, shoving Steven into the wall.

'Knock it off,' Noah yelled. 'We've got bigger problems.' He paused, waiting for Martha and Daniel to notice what had happened. They shone their lights around the room more than once before Martha could be seen to silently mouth the word *impossible.* 'Right,' Noah continued, trying to keep calm, 'I guess as we can all see what's happened, even if it makes zero sense. So, I'm not dreaming, unfortunately. Now, I can't even begin to comprehend how this has happened, but the only way out must be through that door. Anyone disagree?' The others simply shook their heads silently, eyes fixed on the small doorway that had appeared. Noah made his way towards it, summoning the courage to touch the brass handle. It turned easily, and the door was pulled open with a creak. The door was no more than three feet in height and led into a tunnel which was drenched in darkness, the roof of which was just as low. The group each shone their torches into the tunnel, reluctant to be the first to enter.

'I don't see how we have any choice,' Martha stated glumly. 'But one of you brave men can go in first.' Having assumed a slight leadership role, Noah took to his knees and made his way in first. The tunnel seemed to wind to the right, so it was impossible to see more than a few feet ahead. Steven followed, then Daniel, with Martha taking up the rear. Noah stopped suddenly and called to the back of the line.

'Martha, can you wedge the door open with something? I don't fancy getting shut in.' Before Martha could reply there was a slam, as though Noah's suggestion had been heard by some unseen force. 'Shit!' Noah exclaimed. 'Is there a handle on this side?' Martha did her best to turn in the confined space and managed to shine her torch in the direction of the now closed door.

'No handle, Noah. No door either,' Martha said. This got everyone's attention, the other three trying to see if what Martha had said was true. Lights shone onto what now appeared as a plain wall, a dead end to the tunnel they found themselves crouched in.

'Anyone feel like we're being herded somewhere?' Steven asked, clearly shaken by the experience. No one replied, as Noah began moving forward. Time became hard to keep track of as they crawled in the darkness. They felt as though hours had passed, but it could just as easily have been minutes. The curve of the tunnel didn't change for some time, not until the concrete walls became mud. The dampness was unwelcome, but it coincided with a steady increase in height which eventually meant the group could stand, albeit a little hunched. There was no doubt that they had been led, or herded as Steven had described it, well into the hillside. Noah came to a stop, the rest of them close behind. They had reached a junction, the tunnel splitting ahead of them. Both directions looked to be identical, and it would be pure guesswork as to which way to choose.

'Left, or right?' Noah asked.

'No idea. It'll probably change before we know it anyway,' Daniel said glumly.

'Shhh,' Martha interrupted, more loudly than she meant to. 'Do you hear that?' Everyone remained silent, trying to tune in on whatever Martha thought she could hear. 'It sounds like...'

'Footsteps,' Steven said, finishing her sentence.

'Should we run?' Daniel asked, eyes wide with fear.

'Fuck that. If someone else is in here then maybe they know what is going on. And if they aren't friendly, then we probably outnumber them. I say we wait.' Noah took a position in front of the group, largely in order to protect Martha, but Daniel was pleased with the opportunity to slink behind the other men. The footsteps were unmistakable now, having trudged from the concrete floor into the wetter, muddy part of the tunnel. The group gasped as one, as a pair of men rounded the corner dressed in what looked to be soldier's uniforms, rifles in hand. Their voices were faint, but the two men were clearly in conversation, and didn't seem to have noticed the four people stood nearby. Noah was about to speak as the soldiers became ever closer, but thought better of it, choosing instead to move against the wall with the others. The group watched as the soldiers disappeared down the tunnel to the right. No-one made a sound until the footsteps had faded to nothing. 'I did just see that, didn't I? Fucking soldiers?'

'I don't know what they were,' Noah said. 'But it certainly looked like that. I think we should head the same way. They didn't even see us, so I can't imagine we are in any danger.'

'Not in danger?' Daniel replied, incredulously. 'Doors vanishing and doors appearing, trapped in a fucking concrete box, then lost in a muddy tunnel with weird soldiers, but not in danger?'

'Noah's right,' Martha said. 'We should follow. I don't see any other options.' Steven agreed, and democracy overrode Daniel's reluctance. With renewed purpose, the group followed in the direction that the soldiers had headed, hoping to gain some clarity to their situation.

There was no sign of the two soldiers that they had seen, but the tunnel opened out into a room which looked very much inhabited. Four sets of bunk beds were lined up against two of the walls, with green backpacks, water canteens, and tinned foods dotted around. On the beds were revolvers, bayonets, and boxes of ammunition. Scattered about the room were open cannisters of something that no-one recognised, but the warning label on the side suggested they steer clear of those. Daniel, especially, was relieved that the room appeared deserted.

'This must have been where the soldiers set up during the war. I'm pretty sure these pill boxes were used in World War II, to keep an eye out for invaders coming by sea,' Steven informed the group.

'Yeah, but I wasn't aware of any actual attempts to land here,' Daniel said.

'So?'

'So, what's the deal with these guys then?' Daniel asked. 'And how come they haven't spotted us yet, if they are keeping watch for invaders?' It was a fair question, but one which brought on a greater sense of dread, and only led to more questions. From the room in which they stood, there was only the option to go back the way they had come, and try the tunnel to the left, or to go straight ahead, through an opening in the muddy wall between the bunk beds.

'If we're trying to catch up with those people we saw, then they must have gone straight ahead,' Martha suggested. No-one disagreed and, torches shining, Noah took the lead into the darkness beyond.

As the foursome progressed along the corridor, no sound could be heard aside from the slow dripping of water coming from somewhere ahead of them. The tunnel narrowed, so that it became a tight fit just to get through, but they trudged on, unaware of wait lie in store for them. Gradually, the walls became further apart, widening steadily, until they found themselves in yet another man-made, underground cavern. It looked exactly as one would imagine a war room to look; a large table in the centre with a map laid out, carved wooden pieces depicting tanks, aircraft, and so on, placed strategically across it. Martha remained at the back of the line and was only two steps into the room when she felt the sting of a bayonet being pushed against her neck.

'Noah,' she whimpered, afraid to turn around. The three men turned quickly, only to find rifles with bayonets pointed at their faces, stunning them into silence.

'What is your purpose here?' one of the soldiers asked. 'This is a military outpost, not an area for playing about in.' Four more soldiers were gathered around, armed and seemingly keen to use their weapons.

'We were sheltering in the pill box. There was a storm, still is, probably. Then things got weird, we went through a small door and ended up here.' The soldiers looked at each other, unconvinced by Noah's explanation.

'More to the point,' Steven interjected. 'What are you guys doing here? I mean, there can't be any danger of invaders coming by sea, can there?' Steven gave a short laugh, but the soldiers looked unimpressed.

'Of course, there is a risk of that. Why do you think we have been put here? And how do we know that you lot aren't those invaders, eh? Turning up in those strange clothes. Could easily be Germans.'

'Germans?' Steven queried. 'There's been no threat from the Germans since 1945!' The soldiers looked at each and laughed, but their laughter contained a hint of confusion, fear even.

'Well, hopefully this whole bloody mess will be over by 1945. But that's a couple of years away still. You lot seem mighty confused.'

'Okay, you guys obviously think you're pretty funny,' Daniel said, now beginning to lose his temper. 'The year is 2018, and I don't know how you did that thing with the moving doors, but we need to get out of here.' The soldiers stayed silent, seeming to consider what Daniel had said.

'Prove it,' one of them challenged, smugly.

'Easy,' Daniel replied, pulling his phone from his pocket. There was no signal so far beneath ground, so he could not demonstrate the wonders of the Internet, but the display clearly showed the time, date, month, and year.

'What the bloody hell is that thing?' the soldier asked, amazed by the piece of technology before him. His face now showed worry. 'Even if we had been here for that long, which is highly doubtful to say the least, I'd be almost one hundred years old! It's impossible.'

'It isn't actually.' Martha spoke up, her voice quivering as she forced the words out of her mouth. She had it figured out but was afraid that speaking her theory aloud would make it true. 'Come with me.' Martha turned on her heels and led the way through the tunnel, and back to the living quarters of the soldiers. 'What was in those cannisters?' she asked, already knowing the answer. Noah, Daniel, and Steven all looked at the soldiers, waiting for an explanation.

'That would be Tabun, Miss.'

'Which is what, exactly?' Martha asked.

'It's a nerve gas. A new chemical weapon. The higher powers use places like this to store it, in case of any leaks I guess.'

'Leaks?' Daniel asked. 'The fucking lids have been taken off!'

'Well, there is no excuse for language like that! I can see that the lids have come off, and I can't say I had noticed that before. But it would seem no harm has been done.'

'I'm sorry,' Martha whispered, her watery eyes moving from soldier to soldier. They stared back at her blankly, all but one who seemed to understand.

'We're dead, aren't we Miss?' he said quietly. Steven took a step backwards, shaking his head as realisation took a hold on him.

'If they are dead, how come they can see us? How come we can see them, and talk to them?' Tears began to run down Steven's cheeks. 'It's not possible,' he screamed.

'What does he mean?' Noah asked Martha gently.

'I think you know darling. We are all dead.'"

"Well, that was cheerful!" Steven said. "Well done, though. Personally, I prefer a bit more blood and guts, but it was a clever little tale." Daniel nodded in agreement, before tipping the whiskey bottle upside down to drain the final trickles.

"Martha, what did you think?" Noah asked.

"It was good, baby. Quite sad really, but I liked it. And don't worry Steven, if it's blood and gore you like then I have a treat in store for you. You won't forget this story any time soon. Are we all ready?"

"Anyone got a beer I can pinch?" Daniel slurred. "I seem to have run dry." Steven pulled a can from his bag and threw it to Daniel, before opening a fresh one for himself.

"You still okay for a drink?" Steven's question was directed at Noah, who held up an almost full beer can and nodded.

"Now we are ready," Daniel announced, slouching back into his camping chair.

"His skull cracked, as the sharp end of the claw hammer found its target, over and over again, until his head was just a matted mess of blood, brains, and hair," Martha began.

Martha's Story

"Now, you may feel a little sorry for the poor chap whose head is no longer as it should be, but don't. I'm not saying that Karma is a real thing; God knows that bad things happen to good people, and some nasty pricks get away, literally, with murder. But this guy, he had a run-in with Karma, in the shape of my hammer. Before this story moves forward, I need to rewind eight years. This puts me back in my final year of university, summed up by very little sleep, and way too much alcohol. This is when I met Kevin, at a party, when I had consumed enough alcohol to ensure I had absolutely no idea what was going on. I don't remember much about that night, and I know I was wasted, which therefore means I couldn't have consented. And as wild as I was in those days, I would have found somewhere a little more discreet than on a sofa in front of a room full of people. These people, some of whom claimed to be my friends, looking on as Kevin slipped my kickers to the side and fucked me right there." A tear formed in Martha's eye, and she looked at the ground. The rest of the group looked at each other nervously, unsure what to say.

"Are you okay?" Noah asked. "This is just a story, isn't it?"

"Of course it is," Martha replied, forcing a smile. "As if I've bashed someone's skull in with a hammer!"

"I didn't mean that bit," Noah said, his concern apparent. Martha reached across and placed a hand on his.

"Just a story," she confirmed.

"Anyway, I never saw the bastard again, and the incident was never spoken about. I knew I was wasted, and I knew these things happened all too often. But it haunted me; I saw his face in my dreams, when I tried to have sex willingly with a partner I would freeze up. I worried that I would never truly be over it. Then, only a few months ago, I saw him on the television. Some piece on the local news about how he had been found guilty of taking photos under the changing room doors at a swimming pool; he'd been given community service and put on the sex offenders register. I had tried to excuse what he did to me, up to this point, blaming myself for my short skirt and drunkenness, assumed he was also wasted, put it down to a mistake made in youth. But this news article proved he had not changed, and there could well be a whole list of victims out there. So, I found him.

It wasn't remotely difficult, thanks to Facebook. I sent him a friend request, which he accepted almost immediately. I then dropped him a message, asking how he was doing, keeping it light, you know? His replies to begin with were short. I expect he was wary of my intentions, but once I brought up that night, told him I didn't hold any grudges, and that my only regret was not being able to remember it well enough, he started to loosen up. Two days later we met up for coffee. I almost backed out of it at the last minute, unsure if I had the strength to face him, but I managed. We had two coffees, before moving onto something stronger, and then made our way back to his flat. It was so easy that it made me realise just how much we trust people not to do us any harm, every day. He poured some drinks and sat on his sofa, whilst I went to the bathroom to freshen up. I returned a few moments later with the hammer, which had been stored in my bag, hidden behind my back. As he heard my footsteps approach, he turned to face me, catching a glimpse of the metal a split second before it struck. There was a wet cracking sound as the first blow knocked him to his knees on the rug, which fortunately was already red in colour, and I stood over him taking in his shocked expression.

He was clearly in pain, and it was a serious injury, but probably wouldn't have been life threatening. The same couldn't be said for the next few moments of frenzied attack, the hammer moving further into his head with every swing until a large pool of crimson surrounded a heap of skull fragments. I wasn't planning to dispose of the body, and I didn't especially care if I got caught, but I took a few steps to conceal my actions. I cleaned my skin of any blood spatter, as well as washing the hammer as best I could. I tipped away the drinks and washed the glasses thoroughly. This was the only suggestion that Kevin had had any company, apart from his newly rearranged skull. My clothes were a mess, but the long coat would conceal them until I could dispose of them away from the scene.

After this I felt cleansed. The nightmares stopped, and I felt as though I had achieved something worthwhile. All I could hope was that the news of Kevin's death would be a comfort to any more of his victims. What I didn't expect to feel was a thirst for more bloodshed. A need to kill again. I mean, killers are bad people, aren't they? That's what we are raised to believe. But what if some people just deserve to die? What if the world is genuinely a better place without them in it? It got me thinking, and it gave me an objective.

I began scouring newspapers for similar stories to the one which had led me to Kevin. They were much less common, at least locally, than I had expected. So, I joined some groups online, under a fake name, of course, and chatted with other victims. I had struck gold, there was no doubt of it. These women, and some men, were angry, vengeful, broken people. People that I could help in more ways than just listening to their horror stories.

Jonathan was my second. He had followed a fifteen-year-old girl into an alleyway and exposed himself to her. Luckily for her, she managed to unleash a spray of deodorant into his face before running away and had the courage to report the incident to the police. It turned out that Jonathan matched the description of a man who had been flashing young girls for months, and the police were quick to find him. He had never got as far as any physical contact with any of the girls, in as much as anyone had reported, and received an almost identical punishment as Kevin had - community service, and his name on a register. Whether Jonathan was already a rapist or not, it would only be a matter of time before he became one. Prevention is the best cure, of course, but I was undecided as to whether he deserved to die. I chose to up my game with Jonathan.

He was easy enough to find, the newspaper having printed his address, only omitting the actual house number. A few sweeps of the street later and there he was in a grubby T-shirt, baggy jogging bottoms, and looking thoroughly dishevelled. He would never fall for it if I suddenly began flirting with him, and I did not know with any certainty if he lived alone. I watched him leave for his community service assignment each morning and return home around the same time each evening for three days. On the fourth, I positioned myself at the entrance to an alleyway, short skirt, skimpy top, near-empty bottle of vodka in hand. I hadn't drunk the vodka, of course, but it gave the impression that I had, especially as I slumped myself to the ground, my back against a small wall. Thankfully no-one passed me before Jonathan, and even he looked as though he was going to keep walking by.

'Hey,' I called out. 'Do you have any cigarettes?' I did my best to sound drunk, and it seemed to work. Jonathan looked around nervously, aware that he shouldn't be even talking to a young drunk girl. Convinced that the coast was clear, he approached me and fumbled in his pockets before pulling out a tin of loose tobacco. He tried to pass it to me, but I told him I was too hammered to roll, and asked him to do it. He obliged, his eyes all over me. 'Drink?' I asked, lifting the bottle towards him. He handed me the cigarette in exchange for the bottle and took a swig of the vodka, still glancing around.

'Thanks,' he muttered, passing the bottle back.

'I really don't think I should have any more,' I told him. 'You may finish it, kind sir.' I put on a giggle. 'Would you like to have a seat?' I motioned to the dirty ground beside me. Jonathan hesitated.

'There's a bench, through the alley. We can sit there, if you want? Then I should get you a cab.'

'My hero!' I declared, pretending to struggle to my feet. He was quick to take my arm and help me up, all the while checking that no-one could see him. I can only assume that the neighbours had all heard about his indiscretions and would be keeping an eye on him as best they could. We were maybe half way along the alley when I shoved him against the fence which ran along one side. I looked a little afraid, until I smiled and rested by hand against his groin. I immediately felt movement and could tell that he was not going to refuse me. By the time I had unbuckled his trousers, he was fully erect, still looking from one end of the alley to the other, fearful of being seen. Of course, I was also concerned about us being interrupted, but for a very different reason.

I made eye contact with Jonathan, trying to look as seductive as I could. Slowly, I dropped to my knees, licking my lips. One of my hands kept a grip on his manhood, whilst the other reached into the side of my shoe to retrieve the scalpel. I had planned to slice the thing off, hopeful that he would bleed out where he lie, but was unsure if this was possible. His penis was thick, and he could potentially overpower me before I caused enough damage. Instead, I chose to stab above it, in the abdomen, as I pulled at his cock. It took a moment for the pain to register, and I sliced horizontally before he could push me away. I fell backwards, watching the thin line that I had created begin to flow crimson. Instinctively, Jonathan placed a hand over the wound, trying to pull up his trousers with the other. I feared he may get away, may even survive, and that simply would not do.

I jumped up from my position on the floor and managed to land two swift jabs with the scalpel into his throat. He took two steps before dropping to the floor, his life draining from his neck and abdomen. As casually as I could manage, I exited the alley from the end opposite to that which I had entered, crossed a small field, and hopped on a bus to anywhere away from the crime scene. This had now become my agenda, my mission, if you like. To rid the world of men who felt it was acceptable to prey on women and children. I began to search for another victim, but much further away from home this time. Although I had used different methods to dispatch Kevin and Jonathan, it wouldn't take the police long to find a connection."

"Sorry to interrupt," Daniel said, "But I must go to the little boy's room." He pulled himself up from the camping chair and wandered towards the tree line.

"Any truth to this story?" Noah asked, still looking concerned about Martha.

"What that I'm a serial killer picking off sleazy men?" she replied with a laugh.

"You know what I mean, the stuff about being at uni?"

"It's just a story," Martha said, but her face told a different story. "What I do know, though, is that pretty much every guy I've met has done something he shouldn't. Whether it's taking advantage of someone, sending dick pics, trying it on with someone they shouldn't." Noah seemed about to say something but thought better of it. He tried to recall any times that he had behaved badly and came to the realisation that he wasn't entirely innocent himself.

"Maybe so," Steven interjected, "But I know plenty of women who behave just as badly."

"Plenty of women?" Daniel scoffed, returning from his trip to relieve himself. "I didn't think you knew any women?"

"Funny man," Steven replied.

"Carry on, Martha," Daniel suggested. "Tell us more about your man-hating serial killer." Martha did not look impressed.

"I wouldn't call her man-hating, more disappointed with men. Anyway, does anyone need a drink before I continue?" The three men looked around at each other, before Noah informed them that he was out of beers.

"My drink ran out a while ago," Daniel stated, before looking at Steven.

"I've got half a can, but it's my last," Steven replied.

"Well, it's a good job I have some more then!" Martha told them, dashing to her tent and returning with a half bottle of tequila. She passed the bottle to Noah to open, before suggesting that they drink from the bottle and keep passing it around. No one seemed to object, and so Martha picked up her story.

"The groups that I had joined online became alive with talk of the murders as soon as news broke. It appeared that nobody had any sympathy for the supposed victims, and the comments were filled with praise for the killer. This only served to validate my agenda. Someone even suggested how great it would be if the killer was part of this group, if there was a way of providing names for him or her to add to the list of targets. I smiled to myself when I read this, seeing how useful this source of information could potentially become. Of course, if one user could suggest that link then the police would be quick to follow, but in a group with over two thousand members, and the alias I had used to sign up, it would be long process to pick me from the line-up.

People began throwing names out, requests for a revenge they were too weak to take themselves. My only comment was a request for proof, along the lines of *'if the killer was to actually read this, surely they will need evidence? Otherwise you could start naming anyone you had a grudge against.'* A few sensible members agreed with me, some thought I was being ridiculous. Then it came -

the evidence. Screenshot after screenshot posted by a user called *Fran75,* allegedly photographs that she had found on her husband's phone. The first showed a woman without clothing, wrists and ankles bound, with three men standing around her. The pictures became more and more graphic, as each of the three men took it in turn to rape the woman. The comments grew like wildfire, with shock and disgust being the dominant reactions. I waited, reading the comments but not adding to them, until someone asked the important questions; *Is this you in the pictures? Is one of the men your husband?*

There was no reply to this question directly, until the following day. *Yes, it is me in the pictures. None of the men are my husband, because he was taking the photographs. He gave three of his friends' permission to do this to me, after losing a game of poker.* More information came from *Fran75,* including the fact that she was still married to this monster, too afraid to leave. She begged someone to make him disappear, and her agony brought me to tears. I knew this would be a huge risk, but I sent her a private message, asked her to meet me for a coffee, and told her I may be able to help. I didn't know if she would show up, but she suggested a place, thankfully over two hours from my home, and a time.

She showed up, on time, and we talked for hours. I listened as she explained the way he had treated her, how he would change from wonderfully romantic to an animal, and then back again. I could see how damaged she had become at his hands, and how desperately she wanted to be free from his control. And then she asked me outright, catching me off-guard.

'You're the one who killed that man in the alley down south, aren't you?' she said in a whisper. Of course, I denied it, but she knew. 'I won't tell anyone, but can you help me?'

'If you can have revenge, and I do believe you deserve it, would it be against just your husband, or all of the men involved?' I asked.

'All of them,' she said with certainty. 'I mean, Tyler was the instigator, but if his friends weren't such scumbags then they wouldn't have gone along with it. I almost sent the pictures to each of their wives but thought they would be better off not knowing.' I felt a bond growing between us and, as cautious as I was trying to be, there was no denying that *Fran75* knew who I was.

'Would you want to be involved?' I asked. She looked surprised, and then appeared to consider the question.

'I don't honestly know. Part of me wants them to suffer, and to know why. But it is a scary thought,' she explained. I understood and chose the moment to offer a deal. A plan that would see us both getting what we wanted and would ensure that I was not at risk of being exposed to the authorities.

'Think about it,' I told her. 'If you want to have them dealt with then I can help, but we do it together. And we find a way to get to them all at the same time.' She nodded her head slowly, thinking it over. 'And when it's done,' I continued, 'I need your help with another problem.' I stood up to leave. 'I'll get a place to stay nearby tonight, so call me when you have decided what you want to do. If I haven't heard by midday tomorrow, I'll be heading home.' I slipped her my number and left the cafe, confident that *Fran75* would be calling soon.

It was almost midnight before my phone rang, just as I was slipping off to sleep. *Fran75* had returned home after our meeting, drank an impressive amount of gin, picked a fight with her husband, and had tried to walk out of the house. He had grabbed her, pushed her, taken her keys, and effectively held her prisoner. What he hadn't thought of doing was taking her phone; a fatal oversight on his part. She had clearly been crying, and was talking quickly, in hushed tones so that he would not hear her. As she continued rambling, a plan began to form in my mind. I was concerned that her enthusiasm for revenge would wither in the morning, once the courage she had gained from the gin had worn off, so I decided we should act immediately.

'Is Tyler asleep?' I asked.

'Probably,' she replied. 'I'm in the spare room now. I was thinking about finding the keys once he was sleeping, so I could leave.'

'You don't need to leave, not yet, anyway,' I told her. 'But you will need to find the keys. And his phone.' I relayed my idea to *Fran75* and she listened in near silence, only speaking to confirm that each aspect was possible to carry out.

'Do you think they will all come?' I asked, once I had explained everything.

'Probably. They are pretty close, and as it's Friday night they will most likely be out somewhere local.' Our conversation ended, and I gave *Fran75* half an hour to put things into motion before I arrived at her home. I took a cab, getting out at the far end of the road so that I could approach the house in silence. *Fran75* opened the door quietly as I approached, allowing me to slip inside.

'Found the keys then?' I asked, despite the answer being obvious.

'They were under his pillow. He's been on the whiskey so is out for the count now.'

'And his phone?'

'All done. Two replies saying they will round at 1am, nothing from Paul.' It was a little disappointing, but Paul may just turn up without feeling the need to reply. 'Can you deal with Tyler?' she asked me, nerves getting the better of her. I had expected this, and I knew that there was no turning back now. I was led to the kitchen, from which I selected the largest of the knives in the block, and we crept upstairs. I ended Tyler quickly, fearful that the large man would be too strong for even the both of us, and his reaction could put us in a dangerous position once his friends arrived. A slit throat is messy, but it is fast. *Fran75* stared transfixed, no emotion showing, no tears and no smile.

Next, I was led to the wardrobe and handed a dress. It wasn't an especially slutty looking one but was certainly short enough to be eye-catching. *Fran75* popped to the en-suite bathroom to tidy up her face, changed into something more revealing than she had been wearing, and led me downstairs to the living room. It was a big space, dominated by a large corner sofa. It was more than big enough to lie on and had a familiarity about it. *Shit,* I thought. *This is where it happened.*

Fran75 disappeared to the kitchen and returned with a tray of glasses, and two decanters. One contained a clear spirit, which I assumed to be gin. The other looked like it contained either whiskey or brandy.

'Don't touch the whiskey', I was told. 'That's for the boys.' I knew what was happening and was impressed that this woman who had appeared so broken earlier, was coming through with my plan. *Fran75* was fetching some tonic water when there was a knock at the door, so I chose to answer it. Two men stood there, both tall, traditionally handsome, almost cheeky looking. They immediately made me think of older versions of high school jocks from American movies. They were surprised to see me, of course, but looked me up and down admiringly.

'Come in,' I told them, before turning on my heels and heading back to the sofa.

'Where's Tyler?' one of the asked, looking through to the kitchen from which *Fran75* was appearing.

'He'll be down soon,' she told them.

'So, what's going on?' the other man asked, still staring at my legs. 'And who are you?'

'This,' *Fran75* said, 'is Lisa.' Without any further explanation, she sat beside me on the sofa, and began running a hand up and down my exposed thigh. We had the full attention of these men now. Without it being offered, one of the men poured himself a large glass of whiskey, the other following suit. *Fran75* explained she would check on Tyler, to see how long he would be, and disappeared upstairs. She must have waited on the landing for a few moments before running back down. 'It looks like he's going to miss the fun, poor baby must have been tired.'

'And what fun is that?' one of the men asked, clearly uncomfortable without Tyler being there to orchestrate things.

'Just some drinks,' I offered. 'And then I suppose we'll see what happens.' I grinned at the men as I poured myself a weak gin and tonic, motioning for them to refill their glasses. They were on their third large whiskeys when the pills took effect. Before we knew it, they were out for the count. This time *Fran75* was more eager to get involved, and we slit one throat each at the same time. There was no getting away from the fact that she would be the prime suspect, regardless of how well we cleared up evidence that we had been there at that time. The photos that I'd seen online had now been printed and were distributed across the sofa. As much as this implicated her further, it did, at least, give an explanation as to why they had died. In a way it was a good thing that Paul didn't show up that night. He could easily be identified in some of the photographs and would be spending a long time in prison very soon."

Martha paused, looking around at the men. For a few moments no one spoke, Steven and Daniel passing the tequila back and forth.

"You are a scary bitch, Martha," Daniel announced with a chuckle.

"Is that the end?" Noah asked. "It's just that *Fran75* was asked to help with some problem, in exchange for taking out her husband."

"Ha, plot hole!" Steven laughed. Martha looked stern.

"That was the story so far," Martha replied, carefully. "Would you like to hear the rest?"

"Maybe," Daniel said, beginning to feel sleepy.

"In that case, I'll hand you over to *Fran75.*" The men looked at Martha, and each other, quizzically. As if from nowhere, a voice appeared behind Daniel and Steven.

"Hi boys." As they tried to turn in their camping chairs, each of them felt a sharp jab to the neck as *Fran75* emptied the contents of the syringes. Noah tried to leap out of his seat, but the sedative-laced tequila hindered his actions, and he toppled backwards onto the damp grass. He felt a sting and looked down to see Martha plunge a needle into his thigh, before being overcome by darkness.

Time to Leave

The three men came around within minutes of one another, finding themselves bound and gagged in Noah and Martha's tent. Whilst Steven and Noah looked terrified, Daniel just looked angry. It was apparent to all of them that Martha's 'story' may have been more than that, with the introduction of *Fran75*. The two women looked pleased with themselves, as they surveyed the pitiful creatures before them.

"Glad to see you're all with us," Martha began, looking from one face to another in turn. "As you may have gathered, the tale I told wasn't all that far from being non-fiction. I embellished a little, of course, for theatrical purposes, but you get the gist. If I'm perfectly honest, I'm not all that pleased with how the story came over. It made me sound like a man-hater, and I do suppose I am becoming one, but I did not want to feel this way. I wanted to move on from the ordeal I suffered at university." Martha glanced at Noah to confirm that his suspicions were correct about this incident. "I hoped when I met Noah that my way of thinking would change, that I may have found one of the elusive 'good men'." Martha snorted a laugh, looking at her partner with disgust. Noah looked confused, trying desperately to establish what he was supposed to have done to disappoint her.

"Don't worry, I'll explain everything," she told him, as if reading his mind. "So, you all know what happened to Francesca here," Martha stated, one hand motioning towards *Fran75*. "Gang-raped in her own home, as a way of repaying her piece of shit husband's poker debt. And you know what happened to those men. Now, we're not saying that any of you have done anything as bad as that, not at all. But..." Martha paused, searching for the best way to explain their predicament.

"You have still all done something reprehensible," Francesca interjected. Martha nodded her agreement. "We have an agenda which is clear from what you know so far, and as much as taking the lives of rapists and perverts may be a part of that, we have been discussing methods more suitable for preventing these incidents taking place to begin with. All three of you have acted poorly towards women at some point in your lives, and this greatly increases the chances that that abuse will escalate at some point. Our intention is to make sure that this does not happen. When Martha explained her plan to me, I felt it would be best to simply cut your throats as we had done to the men before you. But what was missing before, the one thing that I regret, is not having had a chance to tell those bastards *why* it was happening. At least you will all die knowing what brought about your demise." With their impending deaths so clearly stated, the men all began frantically trying to shake their binds loose, to no avail. Martha and Francesca watched with bemused smiles on their faces, enjoying the power they now held. Once the men had given up trying to free themselves, Martha spoke.

"I'll start with you, Noah," she said, her voice confident and clear in the now-quiet of the tent. "I loved you; I fell completely in love with you even against my better judgment." Noah tried to reply but only muffled sounds escaped the gag. "I'll allow you a chance to speak when I have finished," Martha told him. "As I said, I fell in love with you. I thought, honestly, that you were the one. You know, it took almost three months of us dating before I found anything on you. I searched hard, determined, I suppose, to prove that you were good. But you let me down." Still Noah looked confused. "Remember Becky? I think you went to school with her?" Noah's eyes widened a little, just enough to confirm that he knew who Becky was. "Now, I know you'll say it shouldn't matter to me, as we hadn't even met when you two found each other online. However, it says a lot about your character, and completely changed the way I saw you. I'm sure you are aware of what you did, but for the benefit of the group I will explain. It started with reconnecting online, which led to a few messages about 'the good old days'. The messages became more and more suggestive, with no regard for the fact that

Becky was married at the time. Perhaps you thought it was harmless fun, but if this was the case then you should have stopped when Becky told you to. But you didn't stop, did you? You stalked her online, sent her pictures of yourself, told her husband that the two of you were sleeping together, even though this was a lie. You were obsessed; that's the only word for it. And, with the copies of the messages between the two of you to begin with, he believed you. What were you thinking? That he would leave her, and she'd come running to you? Well he did leave her." Martha looked around the group, all of whom were listening intently.

"Becky found him hanging in the garage, unable to cope with his wife's infidelity. You took a life which did not deserve it, you ruined a family, and for what? I hope you think it was worth it." Martha only now noticed that tears had begun falling from her face, genuinely upset for the death of a man she had never met. She crouched over Noah, removing his gag. "Anything you'd like to add?"

"It sounds like you know it all," he said, his eyes watering, a look of guilt and sadness on his face. "That's what happened. I'd always liked her at school, and I wanted her. No, I didn't care that she was married, but I was young and was being a prick. It's never happened again, and I feel awful for it. But it's too late for me to change any of that now."

"Yes," Martha agreed. "Yes, it is." Pulling the scalpel from the side of her shoe, she held it to Noah's throat. The cold blade felt threatening against his skin, his eyes pleading with Martha to spare him. "Goodbye," she whispered as the blade made its mark, dark red blood flowing freely as Noah tried impossibly to breathe. In a few seconds, he was gone.

This event had sparked a renewed vigour in Steven and Daniel, now certain that it was fight or die. Nevertheless, no matter how hard they tried, the two men could not release themselves from the restraints. Their seemingly feeble attempts to free themselves were brought to an end by the mallet that Francesca wielded connecting with Daniel's left knee. There was a nauseating crunch, followed by Daniel's muffled scream. After a few moments, Martha once again had the attention of the group.

"As you're making the most racket, I'll get to you next," Martha told Daniel. "At least you should be aware of what you did to end up here, eh? I mean, it has been going on since you started working in that office, and I doubt you've seen the errors of your ways." Daniel looked at Martha and she thought she could detect a smirk beneath the gag in his mouth. *Smug prick fucking knows, and doesn't care even now,* Martha thought. *I'll take my time with this one.* "So, for Steven's benefit, as he might not be aware of the 'game', there is something called 'hot or not' that shitty teenage boys sometimes play in school. It's essentially a rating system for girls, like giving them a mark out of ten. Pretty mean, but I wouldn't punish a fourteen-year-old for that behaviour. How old are you, Daniel? Thirty-two? Thirty-three? You really should know better. But Daniel hasn't been playing 'hot or not', have you?" Martha made her way to her bag and pulled out a printed sheet of paper, holding what looked like a spreadsheet up for Daniel and Steven to see.

"Bitch Bingo!" Martha announced with disgust. "Now, I know how it's played, Daniel, but I'm going to take the gag out and let you explain. Make sure you tell us all the rules, or there will be a consequence." Martha bent down to removed Daniel's gag. She looked at him, waiting for him to begin.

"It's pretty straightforward," he began, not showing any sign of the shame or embarrassment that Martha had hoped for. "The column down the right has the initials of five girls from work. The row across the top are five things that the players have to get the girls to do, in no particular order." Both Martha and Francesca looked disgusted by what Daniel was saying, and even Steven was frowning, surprised by what he was hearing.

"Go on," Martha said.

"And then, if you get one of the girls to do one of the things on the sheet, you get your initials in the corresponding box. Once you have a line of five then you win."

"So, let me make sure I understand," Francesca piped up, taking the sheet from Martha. "You can win by either getting one of these girls to do all five acts, that's a kiss, a hand job, a blow job, sex, and nudes? What does nudes mean?"

"Send nude pictures," Daniel replied, his confidence starting to show signs of cracking.

"Or, you can win by getting each of the girls to do the same thing to you? So, if you got a kiss from all five of them, that would count?" Daniel nodded. "There are three sets of initials in the squares; the players, I assume?" Again, Daniel nodded, knowing where this was heading. "So, one of your colleagues with the initials C.D. has apparently kissed two of these women and had sex with one of them. I assume kissing during sex doesn't count? And B.P. has only managed to kiss one, and she's one that kissed C.D. as well. Do they both get a point for that?" Daniel didn't reply. "What's interesting though, is that the other set of initial, D.G., has got his initials in four of the boxes along the top row, having kissed, slept with, had a hand job from, and received nudes from a woman with the initials K.R. These initials, D.G., is you, right? According to this, you've also had sex with two more of the women on this sheet, but it's confusing me because this is dated as starting only a few weeks ago, meaning this has been going on despite you having a wife, who was pregnant at the time! You're a fucking pig, Daniel."

"Okay," Daniel began, looking pissed off rather than ashamed. "I see how it looks, and it was wrong of me to cheat on my wife, I get that. But the women in the game haven't been made to do anything they didn't want to do; it was just some fun, and I know they enjoyed it."

"Do they know about your little game, though?" Martha asked, already knowing the answer.

"Well," Daniel stammered, "they don't know, but it doesn't affect them." Martha couldn't believe what she was hearing.

"I've heard enough," she said. "Here's what's going to happen now. The women on the list will be told about your game. Your wife will be told as well. The other men involved will be dealt with by us shortly. But first, it's time for you to leave." Daniel's eyes widened in fear, the reality of his fate now sinking in. Even after witnessing the murder of Noah, he had clung to the hope that he could escape with a lesser punishment. It was not to be. Francesca took a knife, much larger than Martha's scalpel, from her bag and straddled Daniel, with one knee either side of him. He tried to wriggle free, to push her off him, but the restraints made it impossible. Using both hands, Francesca held the knife as high as her arms allowed, before plunging it down into the centre of Daniel's ribcage. There was a gurgling sound, as his mouth filled with blood, and an escape of air as the knife was pulled out. Francesca repeated the stabbing motion five more times, until she was satisfied that Daniel was gone.

Steven became frantic, certain that he could not escape, but also positive that he had done nothing to warrant this punishment. He tried to plead through the gag, becoming infuriated that he could not speak clearly.

"Calm down," Martha ordered. "I'm going to take off the gag, so we can talk." Once he was able to communicate freely, Steven begged for an explanation.

"You sent a picture of your penis to a girl you met in a pub," Martha told him. Steven tried hard to remember when this could have been, and it took a few minutes to recall.

"I did," he admitted, sadly. "I was drunk, I thought it was funny if anything. She gave me her number and seemed nice."

"And how did she react?" Martha pressed.

"She told me I was being too forward, and I didn't hear from her again. And I learned from that, although I know I shouldn't have needed to. I've never done it again, and I had never done it before. It isn't like what Noah and Daniel had done. If I'd known they were capable of those things I wouldn't have spent any time with them."

"Do you think they got what they deserved?" Martha asked. Steven was unsure how to answer. Of course, murder is wrong, regardless of what the person has done. But he could see why these women had responded in this way.

"I think Daniel would not have changed his behaviour, even if he had been caught by his wife, or his employers, so yes, perhaps he did deserve it. Noah seemed genuinely remorseful, and if I'm completely honest, I think he had been punished enough with the guilt of what happened to that Becky's husband." Steven waited for Martha to speak, hoping that his honesty would go in his favour. Martha and Francesca whispered among themselves for a few moments before seeming to have come to a decision.

"We want you to help us," Martha began. Steven looked confused, frowning, but staying silent.

"It would be much easier for us to select the most suitable targets if we had a male accomplice, someone who would be able to learn more from these men. There are so many things that these monsters won't admit to a woman, but among themselves they will brag about anything."

"And if I don't?" Steven asked.

"We can't very well just let you leave, can we? But I do believe you have better judgment than, perhaps, we have shown. We don't feel that you deserve to die, so please don't force our hand on that."

"I don't know if I can choose people for you to kill! It's not right, Martha. Surely you can see that?"

"Don't look at it that way," Francesca said, almost pleadingly. "You agreed that Daniel was a danger, that there was no other way to stop his behaviour." Steven gave a small nod. "But you also feel that Noah should have been spared. So, if you were to help us select the targets, if you could give us your opinion of who was redeemable and who was beyond help, then you could be saving more lives than you condemn."

In a roundabout way, the idea made sense to Steven. He was in no position to refuse at that moment, if he wanted to live any longer. He took a minute to weigh up the options. He could refuse, but he would be killed right here with his former friends. He could pretend to agree until the police could be contacted, but did these women deserve to be locked up? He was still unsure about that. Or, the only other option, would be to go along with their plan, hoping that his opinion as to who should be left alone would carry enough weight, and only the worst men, if any, would face Martha's brand of justice. That had to better than letting Martha and Francesca continue down this path, murdering any man who even looked at a woman. Little did he know at the time, but Steven would soon be relishing his part in the women's agenda, getting his own hands even dirtier than theirs, and becoming part of the most prolific serial killer trio in history.

THREE: A SEQUEL TO FOUR, COMING 2020.

Collection I: Embrace the Darkness & Other Stories

Step into the mind of the unstable, where nightmares become reality and reality is not always as it seems. Embrace the Darkness is a collection of six terrifying tales, exploring the darker side of human nature and the blurred line between dreams and actuality.

Collection II: Tunnels & Other Stories

From the author of Embrace the Darkness, Tunnels takes you on six terrifying journeys full of terror and suspense. Join a group of ghost-hunters, dare to visit the Monroe house on Halloween, peek inside the marble box, and feel the fear as you meet the creatures of the night.

Collection III: The Artist & Other Stories

The nightmares continue in this third instalment of short horrors from P.J. Blakey-Novis. The Artist and Other Stories contains a terrifying mix of serial killers, sirens, ghosts, claustrophobia, supernatural powers, and revenge guaranteed to get your heart racing and set your nerves on edge.

The Broken Doll

In a small town in southern England, a chance encounter triggers a catastrophic series of events from which no one will emerge unchanged. When Sebastian Briggs meets Ella, she needs his help. The type of help required, however, is far from what he had expected; dragging him down a path of lust and violence. As a married father of three, Sebastian must fight between his loyalty to his family and the desire he feels for another woman, a woman full of secrets and with sinister intentions. What begins as a simple conversation between two strangers soon escalates beyond any expectations, tearing apart Sebastian's home life and leaving death in its wake. The debut novel from P.J. Blakey-Novis is a fast-paced tale, full of twists, crimes and steamy passion.

The Broken Doll: Shattered Pieces

After trying to outrun his problems, Sebastian Briggs is pulled back to his home town to confront his past, with devastating consequences. Having to deal with his estranged wife, and the unstable woman who tore his life apart, Seb discovers that he is now a wanted man; the net quickly closing in with the threat of violence around every corner. Shattered Pieces is the nail-biting follow-up to The Broken Doll, bringing the twisting tale to a shocking climax.

Printed in Poland
by Amazon Fulfillment
Poland Sp. z o.o., Wrocław